What Do You Know About

States of Matter

PowerKiDS press

Tilda Monroe

New York

Published in 2011 by The Rosen Publishing Group, Inc.
29 East 21st Street, New York, NY 10010

First Edition

Editor: Amelie von Zumbusch
Book Design: Kate Laczynski
Layout Design: Ashley Burrell
Photo Researcher: Jessica Gerweck

Photo Credits: Cover, pp. 6, 7, 8, 9, 13, 16, 17, 19, 21, 22 Shutterstock.com; p. 5 Gary John Norman/Getty Images; p. 10 Nick Dolding/Getty Images; p. 11 John E. Kelly/Getty Images; p. 12 Jason Reed/Getty Images; p. 14 Image Source/Getty Images; p. 15 Susie Adams/Getty Images; p. 18 © www.iStockphoto.com/Maurice van der Velden; p. 20 © Javier Larrea/age fotostock.

Library of Congress Cataloging-in-Publication Data

Monroe, Tilda.
  What do you know about states of matter? / Tilda Monroe. — 1st ed.
    p. cm. — (20 questions: physical science)
  Includes index.
  ISBN 978-1-4488-0670-6 (library binding) — ISBN 978-1-4488-1246-2 (pbk.) — ISBN 978-1-4488-1247-9 1(6-pack).
  Matter—Properties—Juvenile literature. I. Title.
  QC173.36.M66 2011
  530.4—dc22
                                          2009053056

Manufactured in the United States of America

CPSIA Compliance Information: Batch #WS10PK: For Further Information contact Rosen Publishing, New York, New York at 1-800-237-9932

Contents

States of Matter

Do you know what matter is? Matter is what makes up everything in our world. Your kitchen table and the milk you drink are matter. The steam your breath makes on a cold morning is matter, too. You may have noticed something about matter. It is not always the same! In fact, there are three main states of matter. These are solids, liquids, and gases.

You may know more about the states of matter than you think you do. When you help bake cookies or put water on the stove to boil, you are causing matter to change states.

When you make cupcakes, you cause matter to change states. Cupcake batter is liquid when you put it in the pans. It becomes solid after you bake it.

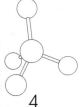

1. What makes up matter?

All matter is made up of tiny parts called atoms. Groups of atoms make up molecules. All matter, whether it is natural or made by people, is made up of atoms and molecules. Atoms and molecules are so tiny that we cannot see them. It takes **billions** of atoms joined together to make the things we see.

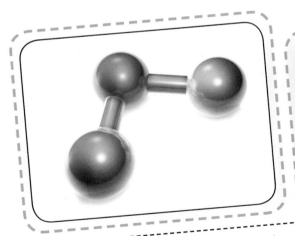

All people need to drink water, as this girl (right) is doing. The drawing above shows a water molecule. Water molecules have one oxygen atom and two hydrogen atoms.

The word "state" describes the form matter takes. One **substance**, or kind of matter, may be found in many states. For example, water can be solid ice, liquid water, or the gas water **vapor**. Different states of matter have different physical properties.

Snow is one example of water in its solid state. It is made up of lots of tiny pieces of ice.

7

Physical properties are the way a substance looks or acts. For example, whether an object floats or sinks in water is a physical property. The **temperature** at which it melts is another physical property.

One of the **characteristics** of all solids is that they hold their shapes. The molecules in a solid are joined firmly together. This makes it hard to make a solid grow bigger, smaller, or change its shape.

Since candies are solid, they hold their shape when you put them in a jar. You can see the space between them if you look carefully.

5. What happens if you break a solid?

Some solids can be broken into smaller pieces. Those pieces hold their shapes, though, since they are still solids.

You can cut up only solids, not liquids or gases. Pieces of a solid, such as bread, will hold their shapes unless you cut them again.

A liquid flows. This means it has no shape of its own. In a liquid, the molecules are close together. However, they are not set in a neat order, as the molecules in solids are. Water and milk are two well-known liquids.

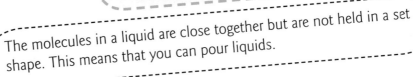
The molecules in a liquid are close together but are not held in a set shape. This means that you can pour liquids.

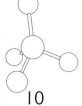

10

When you pour milk into a tall glass, it takes on the shape of that glass. If you poured it into a short, wide glass, the milk would take on that shape. This happens because liquids take the shape of the **container** into which they are poured. Liquids have no set shape. They do have a set **volume**, though. If you spilled milk on a table, it would spread out and drip off the edges of the table onto the floor.

In this photo you can see how liquid water fills a container, such as a glass. It even fills in the spaces between the solid pieces of ice in the glass.

11

8. What are the characteristics of a gas?

Like liquids, gases flow. Unlike liquids, gases have no set volume. This means that gases can fit in a big space or a tiny space. Their molecules just move closer together or farther apart.

Some planets, such as Saturn, seen here, are made of gas. Jupiter, Uranus, and Neptune are other planets that are also made mostly of gas.

Gases spread out as far as they can to fill up any container. Gas can be pushed into a very small space.

The same amount of gas can also fill up a whole room. This makes gases very different from liquids. Could you pour all the water from a large container into a smaller one? Most of the water would not fit in the small container.

When they are underwater, deep-sea divers often breathe air that has been pushed into a tank. It is only possible to do this with air because it is a gas.

Matter changes state when **energy** is added or taken away. Most matter changes because of heat energy. Changes in **pressure** can change matter, too.

This woman is using a very hot flame to melt silver. She can then shape the melted silver into any form she wishes.

The atoms and molecules that make up matter are always moving. Even the molecules in solids are moving, just not very much. When matter is heated enough, the molecules move faster and with greater energy. If enough heat is added, a solid can become liquid and a liquid can become gas. In the same way, molecules slow down when they are cooled. Matter that is cooled to a certain point changes. For example, a liquid becomes a solid.

When things, such as these popsicles, melt, their molecules start moving around more quickly.

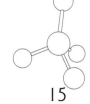

15

12. Will all matter melt?

Gases and liquids cannot melt. Melting is when a solid becomes a liquid. Most solids will melt if heated enough. The temperature at which this happens is a substance's melting point. Some solid matter, such as wood, does not melt. Instead, it burns. This is called a chemical change. Burning changes the matter into a new substance.

Burning wood produces a chemical change. When matter changes states, though, it goes through a physical change.

13. What is it called when a liquid changes into a solid?

When a liquid becomes a solid, it freezes. The temperature at which a liquid freezes is the same as its melting point. Water begins to freeze, or become ice, at 32° F (0° C). If ice is being heated, it begins to melt at 32° F (0° C).

Saltwater has a lower melting point than fresh water does. The saltwater in the ocean freezes at around 28° F (-2° C).

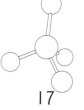

14. When does liquid turn into a gas?

The temperature at which a liquid turns into vapor is its boiling point. The boiling point of water is 212° F (100° C).

15. Do you need to use a stove to turn liquid into a gas?

The heat from the stove speeds up **vaporization**, but it can happen another way, too. Think about what happens to puddles after it rains. Heat from the Sun turns this water into vapor. This is called evaporation.

Milk has a lot of water in it. Therefore, the boiling point of water is also generally 212° F (100° C).

16. Why is the outside of my juice glass wet?

When water vapor in the air hits your cold juice glass, some of the molecules **condense** and the glass gets wet.

This happens because the vapor molecules near the chilly glass cool down. They lose energy. When they cool down enough, they become liquid.

The dew that gathers on leaves, grass, and spiderwebs is another example of condensation. Dew forms because water molecules in the air condense when it cools down at night.

17. Can a solid turn directly into a gas?

Sometimes solids do not need to melt before they turn into gases. When a solid turns directly into a gas, it is called **sublimation**. Frozen carbon dioxide, called dry ice, turns directly into a gas at -109.3° F (-78.5° C).

This scientist is holding dry ice in a test tube. Dry ice is colder than water ice, so scientists use it to keep things very cold.

18. Can a gas turn into a solid?

Yes, gases can turn directly into solids sometimes. This is called **deposition**. One example of deposition is when snow forms inside a cloud. When it is cold enough, water vapor in clouds turns into ice without condensing first.

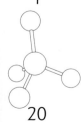

Stars are made up of a fourth state of matter called plasma. Plasma is a gas that has an electric charge. It is not found very often on Earth. It is found in the Sun, lightning, neon lights, and even some TVs.

When lightning strikes, air changes from a gas to plasma. It takes a lot of energy for this change to take place.

We count on liquids, solids, and gases every day. We use water for drinking, to grow crops, and to clean our bodies. We need the gases in Earth's **atmosphere** to breathe. Solids, such as the rocks in Earth's **crust**, make up the very ground on which we stand. The clothes we wear and the homes we live in are solids, too. Understanding the states of matter and the way matter changes between these states is a big part of understanding our world.

People are not the only ones that need water to live and grow. All plants and animals must have water.

Glossary

atmosphere (AT-muh-sfeer) The gases around an object in space. On Earth this
  is air.

billions (BIL-yunz) Thousands of millions. One billion is 1,000 millions.

characteristics (ker-ek-tuh-RIS-tiks) Special features of something.

condense (kun-DENTS) To cool and change from a gas to a liquid.

container (kun-TAY-ner) Something that holds things.

crust (KRUST) The outside of a planet.

deposition (deh-puh-ZIH-shun) The way in which molecules in a gaseous state
  become a solid.

energy (EH-ner-jee) The power to work or to act.

pressure (PREH-shur) A force that pushes on something.

sublimation (suh-bluh-MAY-shun) The way in which molecules in a solid
  become a gas.

substance (SUB-stans) Any matter that takes up space.

temperature (TEM-pur-cher) How hot or cold something is.

vapor (VAY-per) A liquid that has turned into a gas.

vaporization (vay-pur-uh-ZAY-shun) The way in which molecules in a liquid
  become a gas.

volume (VOL-yoom) The amount of space that matter takes up.

23

Index

Web Sites

Due to the changing nature of Internet links, PowerKids Press has developed an online list of Web sites related to the subject of this book. This site is updated regularly. Please use this link to access the list:
www.powerkidslinks.com/quest/sm/

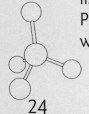